Brothers Grimm

THE MUSICIANS OF BREMEN

ROYDON PUBLISHING Co LTD   81 Goswell Road — London E.C.1

There was once a man, and this man had an ass that had carried heavy loads to the mill for as many years as could not be remembered. But the ass was now rather dispirited at the thought of hard labour, as he was growing weaker and weaker. His master

therefore decided to starve him to death; but the ass, gathering what was in store for him, left slyly to Bremen. It simply dawned upon him that he might be chosen town musician. After he had travelled for some time, he saw a dog lying by the roadside and panting as if he had raced round the whole world.

"What makes you pant so, my friend?" inquired the ass. "Oh, I am but an old wretch, and can no longer chase the game," said the dog, "so my master judged to bring my life to end. I ran away from him; but how can I earn a decent living?" "Hark ye!" said the ass, "I am going to Bremen to become a musician. Come with me, and try your luck." The

dog thought it was a fine proposal, and they headed for the town together.

After some time they met a cat sitting in the middle of the road and looking very upset and sad at heart. "Pray, my good lady," exclaimed the ass "what's wrong with you, you look quite downcast!" "Oh poor me!" replied the cat, "how can I make merry

when the sword hangs over my head? Because I am
growing old and I am beginning to lose my strength,
and I chose to stay comfortably by the hearth rather
than run about after mice, my mistress wanted to
drown me; and though I managed to get away,
I do not know what will become of me and what I
am to live upon." "That!" exclaimed the ass, "join

us to Bremen. You are a peerless night singer, and may earn a fortune in this trade." The cat could not dismiss such an offer, and joined the party.

As they journeyed on, the castaways passed by a farmyard. Perched upon a gate there was a cock yelling out his grief with all his might and main. "Pray what is all about?" asked the ass. "By hook

and by crook you can wake the dead with your noise."
"Ah me!" said the cock, "I was just announcing
that we should enjoy fine weather, and yet my
mistress would not spare my life. All they want to
do is to cut off my head tomorrow, and make soup
of me for the guests that are coming on Sunday. So,
don't you say I waste powder and shot!" "God

forbid!" cried the ass; "come with us Master Chanticleer; it will be better, anyhow, than waiting here to have you head cut off! Besides, if you sing in tune we may all meet with success."

Master Chanticleer was rather taken with the idea: so the four of them set out together. However, they could not reach the town the first day, and, when

night came round, they were obliged to go into the wood to sleep. The ass and the dog laid themselves down comfortably under a tree. The cat and the cock climbed up the tree. Nevertheless, Master Chanticleer was not satisfied till he got to the tree top, as he felt much safer up there. But, as custom is the

second nature, before he went to sleep, he looked
around to make sure that everything was well. In
doing so, he saw far off something shining; then
calling to his companions said, "There must be a
house not far from here, as I can see a light." "If
that is so," said the ass, "it would be better to change

our place, as I cannot say this is the best lodging I
have ever had." "Moreover," continued the dog,
"a bone or two, or a juicy piece of meat would not
ruin my life." So saying, they headed for the spot
where the cock had seen the light; as they drew nearer
and nearer, it became brighter and brighter, till at
last they came to the home of a gang of robbers.

The ass, being the tallest of the company, got close
to the window and peeped in. "What can you see
in there?" inquired the cock. "What do I see?" came
back the answer; "well, I see a table decked with all
kinds of tasty things and the robbers sitting around
it and making merry," "That would be a good place
for us," "said Master Chanticleer. "Yes, indeed"

emphasized the ass, "if we could only get in."

They examined the matter thoroughly and at last hit upon a plan. The ass got himself upright on his hindlegs, resting his forefeet against the window; the dog sat upon his back; the cat climbed on the dog's shoulders, and the cock flew up and got upon the cat's head. Upon a signal, they all began their

concert. The ass brayed, the dog barked, the cat mewed, and the cock screamed; then they all broke in through the window and tumbled into the room with a terrible clatter. The robbers, thinking that some hobgoblin had burst in, fled away as fast as they could.

The travellers sat at the table and ate all the food,

giving no rest to their jaws. Finally, there was no food left and they put out the lights, and each looked for a comfortable and suitable place to spend the night. The ass found a heap of straw, the dog a mat behind the door, the cat a hearth before the warm ashes, the cock a beam on top of the house. As they were very tired, they soon fell asleep.

At about midnight the robbers saw from afar
that the lights were out and all seemed quiet, and
they began to think they ran away for nothing. One
of them decided to go and see what was going on,
and finding everything still, he ventured into the
kitchen feeling his way till he got a match to light
a candle; then, seeing the sparkling eyes of the cat

he mistook them for live coals, and held the match
to them to light it. The cat, not understanding
this joke, sprang at his face, and scratched him.
Dreadfully scared, he ran to the back door; but
there the dog jumped up and bit him in the leg;
then, he set out running across the yard, and the
ass kicked him; and the cock, awakened by the noise,

crowed with all his might. Then, the robber ran as fast as he could, and stopped only before his captain: "That is the end of all of us," he said. "A frightful witch has got into the house. She scratched my face with bony fingers; and a man, who had hidden himself behind the door, threw a knife at my leg; a black monster hit me with a club in the yard; and the devil

himself cried out from the top of the house: "Bring me the rascal!" Hearing this the robbers never set foot in the house again, while the musicians were so satisfied with their home that there they are at this very day.